The Goof That Won the Pennant

Also by JONAH KALB

The Kid's Candidate

How to Play Baseball Better
Than You Did Last Season

The Easy Baseball Book

By JONAH KALB and DAVID VISCOTT

What Every Kid Should Know

By JONAH KALB
The Goof That Won the Pennant

Illustrated by Sandy Kossin

Houghton Mifflin Company

Library of Congress Cataloging in Publication Data

Kalb, Jonah.
  The goof that won the pennant.

  SUMMARY: The young players on a baseball team who are
developing a taste for winning take advantage of a
once-in-a-lifetime error.
  [1. Baseball—Fiction] I.   Kossin, Sandy.
II. Title.
PZ7.K12349Go   [Fic]   76-21678
ISBN 0-395-24834-5

Ida G. Krebs,
master teacher, who knows
that to goof
is to be human

The Goof That Won the Pennant

1

THE GATHERING of the Blazers for the first practice of the season was more like the gathering of a circus than a baseball team.

Roger, for example, came completely equipped with "professional" glove, his own bat, his own helmet, and even his own batting glove.

Joe Ferguson came with both wrists taped — injured, he said, last year. Last year, he had also complained of sprains in both his knees, neck, elbow, and "the little bone below the shoulder on the right side." It was Irky Jacobson who told him that his complaints gave everyone on the team a pain, but not in "the little bone."

Irky himself, though, came with his usual sandwich. "My mother's idea," he once explained. But he never failed to eat it, no matter whose idea it was. Irky was a little overweight. About thirty pounds overweight, to tell the truth.

"Betcha he eats it before the infield drill," Elliot Philo said to J.C. Hall. "Betcha" was Elliot's most important word. He would "betcha" on anything, any time, anywhere. And, of course, "Betcha" became his nickname. But J.C. wasn't interested in the bet.

J.C. was interested in Gale Southworth, who stood in deep centerfield watching. Gale was a junior high cheerleader. J.C. remembered her from football. One day, playing defensive back, he had chased a ball carrier near the sidelines and made the tackle right in front of Gale and the other girls. The girls jumped up, and clapped, and yelled. J.C. didn't know exactly what they were yelling about, but he knew he liked it. Ever since then, he'd been getting his hair cut regularly.

And then there was Baxter Snow, the "phantom" at second base. Baxter was moving right, moving left, making one great imaginary play after another. Play after play he would leap into the air, reach to spear an imaginary ball, and then fire it to first to complete his daydream. He had never done anything like it with a real ball in a real game.

Coach Paul Venuti blew his whistle and gathered the team around him on the grass.

"Look, you guys," Coach Venuti began, "before the season begins, let's decide. How do you feel about trying to win this year?"

"I don't know," said Irky. "We had a pretty good time losing last year." He began unwrapping his sandwich.

"See! See!" yelled Betcha to J.C. "He's eating it!"

3

"We have pretty fair talent," Coach Venuti went on. "I think we might be able to win. But we'll have to try. Does anyone want to try?"

"Betcha we couldn't win anyhow." Betcha this and betcha that. It was a good nickname.

"What do we have to do?" asked J.C. "To try, I mean."

"Well, for one thing," the coach explained, "no more voting about who pitches and who plays where. You've got to let me decide. I'm the coach."

"I'm against that," Irky said, his mouth full. "I liked voting."

Baxter put his fists together, one on top of the other, and swung. His imaginary bat hit an imaginary ball as far as he could see. He shaded his eyes to follow it, way far back over the imaginary fence. "I'm for winning this year," he pronounced.

"If my arm didn't hurt, I bet we could win," Joe Ferguson added.

4

"You're on. Betcha we can't," said Betcha.

"Let's hear from the new kids," Coach Venuti said, bringing the team to order. "What do you think, Roger?"

Roger looked around, and then, suddenly, at his feet. He was on the spot. A direct question meant that he would have to give a direct answer. He didn't like that. He was confused.

For one thing, he never heard of a team that voted on everything. But maybe, he thought, that was his fault. He never was on an organized team before. Still, he thought it sounded weird. In the end, he said nothing. He just looked at the ground, looked at his shoes, and shrugged his shoulders.

It was J.C., shining the top of his baseball shoe on the back of his pants leg, who made the key argument.

"Looky here," he said. "We can always try to win for a little while, anyway. Then, if we don't like it, we can go back to the old way later."

So it was agreed. The Blazers would try to win this year. Coach Venuti was the boss. They would try to play baseball like everyone else.

And they would see if they liked it.

2

THE "NEW PLAN" almost broke down before it ever got started. Coach Venuti told J.C. that he was going to be the lead pitcher, and immediately both J.C. and Joe Ferguson complained.

"Hey, coach," J.C. said. "Pitching gets you all sweaty, and dirty, and stuff. Can't I play centerfield?" He remembered where Gale Southworth liked to stand.

"I was the lead pitcher last year," moaned Joe. "Didn't you like the way I pitched?"

"No, to both of you," said Coach Venuti.

7

Joe sulked. "It's hard to pitch when you're hurt," he said.

"Which is always," said Betcha. Coach Venuti groaned. It looked as if Betcha and Joe *still* didn't like each other — a carry-over from last year.

"J.C. is the number one pitcher. For now, anyway. We'll try Joe as the backup." He then sent the Phantom to second base, Joe to first, and Irky to third, "where you won't have to move too much." Betcha had been the catcher last year, and he was sent there again. Three new kids, including Bunky Strahm, were assigned to the outfield.

"Your father tells me you play shortshop," Coach Venuti told Roger. "Let's try you there."

Roger trotted out to shortstop, sick and happy at the same time. When did his father speak to Coach Venuti, he wondered? Did he call him? "I could have made shortstop without his calling," he thought. "I don't like him to call." Then he got set at his position.

After the first round of ground balls to the infield, it was not at all clear why Coach Venuti thought this team had "talent."

Irky, of course, didn't bend — even a little bit — and the first few balls went right under his glove.

Roger bent. Roger even caught the ball. But his throw to first base had nothing — a weak floater. Joe Ferguson caught it, and yelled "ow!"

Phantom Baxter Snow was more dramatic, but just as bad. The ball was hit right at him. He came charging in like a Joe Morgan, twisted his glove for a backhanded sweep, swept upward, leaped in the air, and fired to first. Unfortunately, he did not have the ball at the time. It had hit his glove and bounced away.

Only J.C. looked cool. "What is the pitcher supposed to do during infield drill?" he asked.

"Nothing," Coach Venuti told him. "Just stand there."

J.C. did that very well. He moved his shoulders back. Then he folded his arms. Finally, he turned his face to third base so that Gale Southworth, still in deep centerfield, could get a look at his right profile.

"Okay," said Coach Venuti. "Let's do it again."

It was about an hour before things began smoothing out — not really too bad for the first practice of the season. Joe complained that the ball hurt him on every throw, but he made the catches anyway. The Phantom tried to look better than he was, but he was still okay. Irky groaned every time he bent. But when he bent, he was a pretty good third baseman. Good hands.

Only Roger continued to show no promise. "Can't you throw harder than that?" Coach Venuti asked him when still another floater finally reached first base.

Roger bit his lip, gritted his teeth, and got ready once more. "I'll show him," he said to himself.

He showed him all right. The next ball Roger threw was high over Joe Ferguson's head, more or less like a fly ball. Coach Venuti turned away so that the boy wouldn't see his smile. "So this is the great shortstop that his father called me about," he said to himself.

After a while, J.C. began pitching to Betcha on the sidelines. Without dirtying his shoes, or rumpling his hair, J.C. still threw a pretty fair fast ball.

J.C. had what is known as a "live" arm. Seemingly without effort, his arm whipped smoothly, and the ball seemed to jump out of his hands. He would have to learn to bend his back more, Coach Venuti thought, as he watched him.

Z-i-i-i-i-ng went another fast ball into Betcha's mitt.

3

PRACTICE IS PRACTICE, but games are games. And even though the Blazers kept getting better in their infield and hitting drills, they had not yet tested themselves against another team.

And they had not yet tested the idea of playing to win.

Coach Venuti had to remind them several times during the three weeks of preseason training that HE, and not they, was boss. Irky was the biggest complainer.

Irky just hated to bend, and when Coach Venuti told him that he couldn't play third base without bending, Irky asked to be put in the outfield.

Instead of that, the coach put him on the sidelines, touching his fingers to his toes, over and over again. Irky grunted, and sweated, and huffed, and complained.

"One more word from you and I'll take your sandwich away," the coach warned him.

"Uggggh," said Irky, as he reached for his toes once more.

But Irky did have good hands at third base. The coach moved him up the line, close in to home plate, to balance off his lack of range. He could pounce on a ball, and throw quickly. He would be fine, the coach thought, if only he would bend.

Roger, at shortstop, was still terrible. Roger really couldn't throw. He cocked the ball near his chin, and sort of pushed it out. He could catch the ball pretty well, though. He just couldn't throw. And throwing is so hard to teach.

But he left him at shortstop anyway.

It was an anxious Opening Day that the Blazers faced. It would be their first try of the new season against another team. And, it would be the first try at the new plan . . . trying to win.

The Cardinals didn't have such fears.

The Cardinals marched in front of the Blazers at the Opening Day parade, and they looked confident.

There were two reasons for that confidence. First, they knew they were playing the Blazers, and that was enough to give any team great confidence. The Blazers, after all, had finished last the year before.

But there was another reason for that confidence, too, although it was harder to explain. The Blazers, even in double-knit uniforms, looked terrible.

Few people besides Coach Venuti knew why the Blazers looked so awful. Irky's double-knit was too small, stretched across

16

his chest and stomach. It simply couldn't hide that extra thirty pounds. Roger's uniform was too big. Betcha's was too tight. Phantom's was so big that the pants reached almost to his ankles. Only J.C.'s uniform fitted him and looked as it was supposed to look.

It was probably a mistake, Coach Venuti thought to himself, as he marched beside his team. But he couldn't do anything about it now.

What had happened, he knew, was that the Blazers had picked their uniforms by the numbers on the back, rather than by the size.

"I want number thirteen," Betcha announced. "It's my lucky number."

"It's the wrong size," the coach told him.

"Who cares?" Betcha replied. "Don't you want me to be lucky?"

That started everybody else. "I want number seven," said Irky.

"I was born on March third," Joe Ferguson announced. "I want three."

Of the whole team, only J.C. said that he wanted a large size, no matter what the number. And as a result, only J.C. got a uniform that fit well.

And as the Blazers turned the corner in the parade, and headed for the playing field, their looks inspired confidence . . . among the Cardinals.

On the field, after "The Star-Spangled Banner" and a few words from the Commissioner, the Chief of Police threw out the first ball (Betcha missed it), and the season officially began.

And the surprises began, too.

With his hat perched gingerly on the top of his head, J.C. fired strike after strike at the knees of the Cardinal batters. His fast ball was live and low. Of the first nine batters to face him, seven struck out, one popped up to Phantom at second base, and the other bounced to Irky at third, who bent, grunted, and made the play. Nobody had reached first base.

Of course, Phantom made that routine pop fly into a "miracle" catch. But he caught it. That was what mattered.

And in the second inning for the Blazers, Joe Ferguson hit a high pitch over the green wall for a home run, and limped around the bases. Everyone knew the limp was baloney. They cheered lustily as he stepped on home plate.

Three innings were gone, and the Blazers were leading 1–0.

In the fourth inning, though, the Cardinals got something started. A ground ball went to Roger at shortstop. He picked it up cleanly, set himself, and then pushed one of those floaters way over Joe Ferguson's head. The Cardinal hitter reached second on the error.

Betcha let a J.C. fast ball get away from

him, and the runner moved up to third. And then, a topped ground ball to Joe Ferguson scored the runner to tie the game.

Nothing more happened until the Blazer fifth — except that everyone knew J.C. was pitching a no-hitter. The Cardinals may have scored a run, but that was not J.C.'s fault. His fast ball was jumping, moving in and out, always around the plate, and always at the knees. He had walked one Cardinal in their end of the fifth, but that was all.

In the bottom of the fifth, with one out, Irky singled up the middle and huffed and puffed his way to first base. Roger, who had struck out twice before, took a mighty swing and topped the ball back to the pitcher.

He might have beat it out. It turned out to be a pretty good accidental bunt. But with Irky on first, waddling his way to second, the pitcher picked up the ball, fired to second, and beat Irky there by four steps. It was just a force out.

Roger went to second on a wild pitch, and was standing there looking important when Phantom popped one up on a late swing. The ball fell over the first baseman's head for a bloop single, and Roger, running at the crack of the bat with two out, came all the way home. Blazers up, 2–1, with only an inning to go.

That bloop hit proved to be the ball game. J.C. adjusted his pants, patted his hair, checked his profile, and threw nine strikes in a row for the three outs. J.C. had his no-hitter, and the Blazers had their first win.

4

COACH VENUTI was hardly through the door of his house when the telephone rang. And before he picked it up, he knew who was calling.

"Hello," said Coach Venuti.

It was Roger's father, just as he knew it would be. Roger's father reported that Roger was upset because of "his little mistake," and didn't realize that he had won the game for the Blazers. He didn't realize that he was the hero of the game.

Coach Venuti didn't realize it either. He asked him how he figured that.

Roger's father explained that if he

hadn't hit that perfect bunt, he wouldn't have been able to go to second on that wild pitch. If he wasn't on second, he couldn't have scored on that bloop single. "The fat boy couldn't have scored on that hit," he added.

Coach Venuti thought he might be right about that, but if Roger hadn't made that two-base error, the Blazers would have won anyway. He said nothing.

"Roger," explained his father, "is terribly upset over that minor little mistake in the field. Could you speak to him? Could you tell him he really was the hero of the game?"

"Sure," said Coach Venuti. "Put him on." Roger picked up the phone.

"Listen, Roger," the coach told him, "you did okay. The big heroes were J.C. for his no-hit pitching, and Joe Ferguson for that super home run, but you didn't hurt us too much. We won, didn't we? You'll get better. Just work hard on getting good throws."

Roger said "Uh," and handed the phone back to his father.

"Thanks," Roger's father told the coach. "I knew you really appreciated him. But he needed to hear it from you. He's standing here smiling now. He's feeling better already."

"Glad to do it," Coach Venuti replied. And he hung up.

5

IT WOULD BE NICE to report that the Blazers were getting better with every game they played, but the truth was, they were pretty lucky in games two and three.

Joe Ferguson pitched the second game because of the league's pitching rules. J.C. couldn't be used again. And the Blazers won it, 8–7, in the last inning when Irky, caught in a rundown between third and home, fell. The Tigers' third baseman, who had the ball, tripped over him and dropped it. Irky got up and waddled home with the winning run.

And in the third game, with J.C. pitching another beauty, Betcha Philo hit a routine ground ball into a comedy of errors against the White Sox. He reached first on an overthrow, went to second on a dropped ball, ran to third when nobody could find it, and scored because the catcher had left his position to locate the ball and nobody covered home.

That was the only run J.C. needed, as he won it 1–0.

None of this may sound like luck, but it really was. Somehow, in neither game, did a single ball go out to shortstop Roger. As a result, he played his position perfectly. No errors. No disappointments. And best of all, no telephone calls from his father.

So after three games, the Blazers had already won more games than they had the entire previous year, and the team took stock.

Did they really like to win? Was winning as much fun as voting? Did they really think they had a chance?

The answers were mixed. It was at a midweek practice that the coach put it to them, and the most he could get from them was, "We'll keep trying for three more games."

J.C. was still worried about all that sweating. But Gale Southworth had come in from deep centerfield, and was now watching the team's games and practices from the grandstand. So he guessed it was all right to keep trying for a while.

Joe Ferguson wanted to go back to the old way. He really didn't like playing first base. All those throws bruised his hand, he said. And besides, he wanted to pitch more. He suggested that he had the votes.

But Coach Venuti thought he heard a little pride in their voices. Three wins were, after all, three wins. He listened only when, and to whom, he wanted, and then announced to everyone that the team decided to keep trying to win for a while. It wasn't as bad as they had thought it would be.

So they went into game four and blew it.

Joe Ferguson was on the mound, and he was wild. And Irky wouldn't bend, and Roger couldn't throw, and nobody could hit and they blew it.

But *how* they blew it was important. After three innings, trailing 4–1, the Blazers began playing like the "old" Blazers . . . as if winning didn't matter. They yukked it up, conceding the game early, and pretended they were having a good time losing. The final score was 14–1.

And after the game, the telephone call.

"When you saw that hurt kid was pitching wild," Roger's father analyzed, "why didn't you try Roger as the pitcher?"

Coach Venuti could hardly believe his ears. Roger as a pitcher? His arm was so weak that the coach was thinking seriously of moving him out of shortstop . . . to an outfield position. But as a pitcher? That was crazy!

"It never occurred to me to use Roger as a pitcher," Coach Venuti told him, truthfully. He didn't care how Roger's father understood that statement.

But the team's return to old Blazer ways really did bother him. Not the loss. Every team loses baseball games. Even the best. But what happened after the third inning upset him. Was this a team that was going to fold every time they got a few runs behind?

And at the next practice, he got tough.

"Listen, you guys," he began. "Every team loses ball games now and then. But you guys gave up! You quit! You didn't play like you wanted to win. That's not part of our agreement."

"Aw, we were going to lose anyway," Irky said, biting into his sandwich.

"I had this awful pain below my left

shoulder," Joe Ferguson reported, "and my stomach was upset, and . . ."

"And you stunk," Betcha interrupted. Joe sulked.

"You weren't so hot yourself," J.C. chimed in. "When I pitched my no-hitter, you didn't . . ."

"Well, I didn't see you doing anything *this* game," added Phantom.

"And what about that kid at shortstop?" cried Irky.

"Hold it. Hold it, everybody. That's enough!" Coach Venuti shouted. Things were getting a little out of hand. You can't have one player criticizing another, he knew. Especially Betcha and Joe. Betcha would use anything he could find to put Joe down.

The team fell silent. Angry and silent.

"I'm the boss, remember? Only I can criticize," Coach Venuti told them after a few moments of calm.

But before the team got up to practice,

Betcha got one more crack in. "Well, you want us to win, don't you?" he asked.

Nobody answered.

And Coach Venuti did a lot of thinking as he drove home that night.

6

DID HE REALLY want the Blazers to win, Coach Venuti asked himself? Did winning matter, at this age, with these kids?

Yes, he decided. Winning did matter . . . a great deal.

He remembered the lesson of his shortstop of a few years before. The boy was in bad shape. He couldn't learn to read in school. One failure after another in school convinced him that there was something seriously wrong with him — something really different. He was sure he was not like other kids, and that he would always fail.

He put him at shortstop, Coach Venuti remembered, and worked with him. The boy could really throw, and really move to the ball. He kept praising him, telling him how good he was. And the Blazers began to win.

Soon, he could see the change in the kid. He stood up straighter, smiled more. He took part in the jockeying on the bench, slowly at first, as if he were testing himself with the other boys. If he thought hard enough, Coach Venuti knew he could name the game, and the inning, when the boy finally decided that he was just as good as anyone else.

Coach Venuti knew that, quite suddenly, the boy's schoolwork improved. He began believing in himself. And as his schoolwork improved, so did his ball playing — one kind of winning helping the other.

Ever since then, the coach reminded himself, he had picked his teams that way.

He went to the league tryouts looking for talent, but looking also for the fat, the shy, the vain, the kooky, the complainer. And at the league draft, he picked them all. Everyone on his team had problems.

If the team was named "The Oddballs," it would have been more accurate than calling it "The Blazers."

Winning, at anything, would help every one of these kids understand who they really were, and what they could do. So why not baseball?

The Blazers of last year, he remembered, were an experiment. He let them vote. He let them do whatever they wanted. He let them decide for themselves. He let them have a "good time."

So what happened?

They decided for themselves, all right. They decided, before the season even started, that they were losers . . . in baseball, just as in everything else. They clowned. They yukked it up. It was so much easier to accept losing if you could tell people that you never really tried. But were they happy? Was it fun?

Behind the laughing, and the yuks, the coach remembered a special sadness. Winning is always more fun than losing . . . always.

J.C. was a really good pitcher. Because of him, a lot of kids who really need it might learn how to win . . . in many things.

Yes, he decided. There was a chance. And so, winning was important, this year, for these kids.

Not at any price. Winning wasn't everything. But it wasn't nothing, either.

He heard the telephone ringing, just as he expected, as he nosed his car into his garage.

7

THE KEY GAME would not be the next one, against the Pirates. J.C. would pitch the Pirates game, and the Pirates weren't very good. The key game would be the one after that — against the Cubs.

Joe Ferguson would have to pitch the Cub game, and the Cubs had a pitcher of their own who could really throw. It was the Cub pitcher who, the year before, won the Town Championship for his team.

Coach Venuti committed the worst sin a manager could commit. He ignored the Pirates during the week's practices, and concentrated on working with Joe for the Cubs game.

"Joe," he told him, "let's think about how a hitter hits. It may give us some ideas about how to pitch."

"Okay," Joe said, "but I'm warning you. This little bone in my knee is acting up, and my left wrist is . . ."

"A hitter has to time the ball, right?" Coach Venuti didn't often ignore complaints, but Joe was a special case. Joe "used" complaints as an excuse for failing.

"So anything you can do to upset his timing is a big help, right?" he continued. "What can you do to upset his timing?"

"Well," Joe said, massaging his elbow, "I can change speeds on the pitches. Throw one hard and one soft. I can throw a fast ball and then a changeup."

"Right," beamed Coach Venuti. "You don't have J.C.'s speed. You can't blow the ball past the hitters. But you can fool them. That's just as good! Mix up the speeds.

Never let a hitter know what the next pitch will be. But there's more you could do."

"More?"

"Sure. Little things that you learn by watching how the hitter stands up there. A hitter tells you a lot, without meaning to."

"Like what?" Joe asked.

"Like if the hitter crouches, he's protecting the low pitch. So pitch him high. Make him hit the way he doesn't want to. If the hitter crowds the plate, pitch him inside. If he steps in the bucket, pitch him outside. He'll never reach the ball."

"I never knew that," Joe said.

"Oh, there's more. If a hitter uppercuts, he can get the low pitches. So pitch him high. If he turns his head, low and outside. If he swings without his hands, pitch him tight. Watch the hitter. He almost always tells you what he can't hit."

Joe worked hard, all week, on the sidelines. He practiced changing speeds on

39

every pitch, and throwing for spots. And not once did he complain of his "pains."

Even if it was a sin to ignore the Pirates, Coach Venuti was right about them. J.C. pitched just hard enough to win easily. Betcha hit his first home run of the season, Phantom got three hits, and the team returned to its winning ways. The Blazers won the game, 8–3. But the Cubs were coming up.

The Cubs were good — no doubt about it. On game day, Coach Venuti watched their batting practice, and didn't like what he saw. Three balls were lost over the green fence in deep left field.

But Joe Ferguson looked confident. He got past the first inning giving up two hits, but no runs.

The game stayed 0–0 for four innings. Each inning the Cubs had something going, but not enough to score. And in each inning, it looked, finally, as if this was the inning that they would really pound Joe Ferguson. But they never did.

Coach Venuti marveled at Joe's poise. In the fourth inning, for example, with Cubs on first and third, Joe struck out one of the big Cub hitters with the slowest slow ball of the afternoon.

Joe Ferguson, the coach told himself, has a great deal of courage. It took guts to throw that pitch, in that spot, to that hitter.

But in the fifth, the Cubs scored a run. For the first time in the game, Joe let the first batter of the inning reach base. An out moved him to second. Joe got the next hitter on a pop to Irky, but then, his luck ran out.

The Cub batter guessed fast ball, and Joe guessed wrong and gave him the fast ball — up high. He drilled it to centerfield, and the runner scored all the way from second without a throw.

"That's okay, Joe," Coach Venuti told him when he came to the bench. "Even the best of us guesses wrong now and then. That's what guessing means. You're pitching a super game."

But he knew that wouldn't help much unless the Blazers could get the run back, and, as it turned out, they couldn't.

The Cubs won the ball game, 1–0, and the Blazers were 4 wins, 2 losses, after the first six games of the season.

The Blazers were down in the dumps. They had lost a tough game. But they hadn't quit. They hadn't lost because they weren't trying.

8

THREE IMPORTANT events happened at the Blazers' next game date.

First, the Blazers stomped the Phillies 11–1, and brought their season's record to 5 wins, 2 losses. J.C. won his fourth game in a row with that smooth, silky, low fast ball.

Second, Roger made three consecutive errors at shortstop. They didn't mean anything to the final score, but he was a problem.

And third, the big news from the other field. The Pirates, somehow, by some magic, had beaten the Cubs, handing them their first loss of the season. The Blazers, it seemed, were not out of the pennant fight yet.

The season was now half over, and the Blazers were comfortably in second place when still another team meeting was called by Coach Venuti.

"Well," he began, "here we are. Second place, one game behind the Cubs. What do you think? Do we go for the pennant? Or do you guys want to go back to voting?"

There was no contest this time. In fact, the team's approval came in the form of a shout. "THE PENNANT," they cried. The fat, the lazy, the vain, the weak . . . the losers . . . liked to win.

But Betcha spoiled it. "We could have been seven and oh, except that Joe lost those . . ."

"Cut it out!" the coach interrupted him. "For one thing, Joe didn't lose those two games. The Blazers did. And for another thing, his game against the Cubs was the best-pitched game of the year." Coach Venuti was angry.

"Hey, wait a minute. How about my no-hitter!" J.C. chimed in.

"No. Joe's game against the Cubs was the best-pitched game. You've got a great fast ball, J.C. You win with that fast ball. Keep it up. But Joe, really, has nothing. Nothing. He pitches with his heart, and with his brains."

"But he doesn't win," added Betcha. He wouldn't let go.

And J.C. was sulking. He went out there and pitched hard, and messed his hair, and got all sweaty, and nobody appreciated him. He'd show him, he thought to himself. He could throw junk, too.

Coach Venuti sent the team on to the field, but called Betcha and Joe to the bench with him.

"All right," he began. "let's talk about it."

"Talk about what?" Joe asked.

"Let's talk about the fact that you two guys don't get along, and that it's hurting the team." Coach Venuti said.

"How does it hurt the team?" Betcha wanted to know.

"Look. A pitcher and a catcher. A pitcher without a fast ball, and a catcher who won't help him. You don't think that hurts the team?"

"Well," said Betcha, "if he . . ."

But the coach went on. "I was going to put in a signal system. I was going to let the catcher call all of Joe's pitches. But I can't do that if you two guys don't get along."

Betcha perked up. "Yeah," he said, "I've got brains, too. I could have called that Cub game."

"Sure you've got brains. And courage. And in this game, two brains are always better than one. If we had a signal system, you could tell Joe what you think he ought to pitch. If he agrees, okay. If he disagrees, he shakes you off. That way, you're both thinking. But I can't do that if you guys hate each other."

"Why not?" Betcha asked.

"Because Joe will start shaking off the *right* pitches, just because you called them. And you will call some wrong pitches, just to see him get hit. And I can't take that chance."

Silence. Thinking.

Joe began. "Well, for one thing, he's always betting . . ."

"And you're always complaining," Betcha flared back.

Joe went on, more quietly. "I don't really care about his betting. I think it's stupid, but I don't really care. But he's always criticizing me. He's always putting me down in front of the other guys. That makes me mad."

"Yeah, well, if you didn't complain so much, maybe . . ." but Betcha stopped

himself. Nobody interrupted. He just decided to think before he spoke. He knew one thing. He really did want to call the signals.

Finally, Coach Venuti spoke again. "Okay, think about it. It's up to Joe. If he wants you to call the pitches, I think it's a good idea. For the sake of the team. But I'm not forcing you."

The two of them ran out on the field and joined the rest of the team. But later on, while taking batting practice, Coach Venuti saw them talking to each other, quietly, behind the backstop. He pretended that he wasn't watching them.

9

THE BEGINNING of the second cycle — the second half of the season — saw the Cardinals back on the field, Joe on the mound, and Roger starting in left field.

Coach Venuti hated to move Roger, but he felt he had no choice. Roger just couldn't hack it at shortstop — at least not this year, on a team that might win the pennant. It just wasn't fair to the other kids.

He broke the news to him gently, and as it turned out, he was more gentle than he needed to be.

"Roger," he said, "I'm going to move you to left field. You're still a starting player, and those three errors in the Phillies game really didn't mean anything. We won. But I think Bunky deserves a shot at shortstop, and I'm moving him in."

Roger's reaction was strange — at least to Coach Venuti. He wasn't exactly happy about the move. He knew, after all, that he had tried and failed. But, at the same time, Coach Venuti thought he saw Roger heave a great sigh of relief.

In fact, when Roger took the field in that first inning, Coach Venuti thought he saw an extra spring in Roger's step . . . as if, secretly, he was glad to be off the hot seat.

Kids always know, Coach Venuti reminded himself. Roger didn't want to lose the pennant for the Blazers just because his father wanted him to play shortstop. He was secretly glad to move to the outfield. Kids always know.

And Joe — Joe — he was still calling his own pitches. He and Betcha couldn't get together — yet.

Joe was pitching his usual game. A little fast, a little slow, a little staggered, a little inside, a little high, a little low. He mixed his pitches well, and the Cardinals, although they got a couple of hits, were doing very little damage.

The Cardinals scored a run in the second, and another in the fourth, but J.C. homered to get one back, and Betcha doubled with the bases loaded for three more.

Joe finished the game by teasing the Cardinal batters. Everything looked so easy, but his pitching to spots was great. Sure, he threw a lot of soft stuff, but never when they expected it, and always to a spot that made it difficult to hit.

The game ended 4–2, and Joe had his second win of the year.

Coach Venuti could hardly believe his ears. "Pretty good game," he heard Betcha tell Joe. It was painful for him to say so.

"Thanks," said Joe. "Pretty good hit yourself with the bases loaded."

There was really no way to avoid the telephone call. It had to come. He knew it had to come. And come it did.

"What do you want me to do?" Roger's father asked Coach Venuti.

"About what?"

"You know 'about what,' " Roger's father exploded. "I've got a very upset boy here, all because of you. Now, I want you to tell me what I should do about it," he demanded.

"Roger didn't look so upset to me. I thought he played a pretty good game."

"Yes, but in left field. You know how he feels about playing shortstop."

Coach Venuti tried to line up what Roger's father was telling him with his own observation on the field. Finally, he got angry. "No, I don't know how Roger feels about playing shortstop. I know how *you* feel about his playing shortstop, but I don't know how *he* feels. And if he really is upset, maybe it's because of you — not me!"

"What does that mean?" Roger's father asked him.

"Look. Roger isn't disappointing me. He's young. And he's new on the team. He'll be okay. But maybe he's disappointing you . . . and that's upsetting him. You asked me what you should do about it. All right. I'll tell you. Lay off. Get off his back. Let him be."

Silence on the other end.

Finally, in a distant voice, Roger's father answered.

"I think, Coach Venuti, that you don't know anything about how to run a team of kids. All you care about is winning. You have no respect for a kid's feelings." And then, he added, "I won't be calling you again."

"Thank you," said Coach Venuti, and he hung up. Hard.

10

J.C. WORKED the Tiger game nice and easy. And Irky left his sandwich home.

Coach Venuti knew that there was something different going on, but he couldn't put his finger on it. And, as usual, it was Betcha, making a wise guy remark, that told him what it was.

"Betcha he forgot it," Betcha said.

"Forgot what? Who?" asked J.C.

"Betcha he forgot his sandwich." He didn't have to say who.

Coach Venuti would have taken that bet. He would have bet that Irky left the sandwich home on purpose . . . maybe, accidentally on purpose. He remembered the strange sight of Irky on the sidelines during the latest practice. Irky was bending, and touching his toes, once, twice, three times. And it was strange because nobody had told him to do it.

In fact, the bending, and the leaving of the sandwich, all seemed part of the "new" Irky. He was moving much better than ever to his left. He was covering that hole between short and third like no other third baseman in the league. And he was moving a lot faster on his hits. The "new" Irky was a very good ball player, He, like the rest of the team, was getting better and better . . . because he wanted to.

But the Tigers were no match for the Blazers in any event. J.C.'s fast ball was low and live, and that's all anyone needed.

Oh, the Tigers got a few hits, but nothing that hurt. And only after the Blazers had the game salted away. The Tigers got their first hit in the fourth when the Blazers were already ahead 8–0. And they might not have gotten even that one if J.C. hadn't been laughing so hard.

What happened was, Mrs. Jacobson came to the game — the first baseball game she had ever seen — and, of course, brought Irky's sandwich with her.

Mrs. Jacobson didn't understand baseball. She didn't know what Irky did all those afternoons at practice, and all those evenings at games. Baseball wasn't anything she cared about.

Still, when Irky saw her there, he felt proud. It's always nice to play for a parent. And in the fourth inning, he made a nice scoop and good throw to get the first out.

But between batters, he was just standing there, hands on hips, and Mrs. Jacobson thought that he was just waiting. And if he were just waiting, wouldn't this be a good time to give him his sandwich?

She left the stands, passed the bench,

passed the third base coach, and held the sandwich out to her son.

Irky could have died. He tried to wave her away, as the umpire called time out. Then, he tried to pretend that she wasn't there. And lastly, he tried to pretend that she was somebody else's mother. But nothing seemed to get through to her.

Irky was about as embarrassed as a kid could be.

Finally, Coach Venuti went to Mrs. Jacobson and led her away, sandwich and all. Nobody knows what he said to her, but she threw her chin back, and stomped her way back to her car. But it was too late for J.C.

J.C. was in hysterics. He was laughing so hard, tears filled his eyes. And although J.C. was not the only one laughing, he *was* the pitcher.

When the umpire called "play ball," J.C. had not yet really recovered. His pitch was not as fast as usual, and it was up a bit, and the Tiger batter laced it into left centerfield.

Roger chased it, made a good play, but it still went for a double. Roger wasn't laughing. Roger know what it was to deal with parents.

So the Tigers were the victims, and the Blazers were rolling again, and at the next practice, Joe Ferguson and Betcha asked Coach Venuti for the signal system.

It was Betcha who approached Joe. "I'm not putting you down any more."

"I know," said Joe.

"In fact," Betcha went on, "I even told the guys you pitched a good game last time."

"I know," replied Joe. He wasn't going to help him.

"Well . . . how about it? The signals."

"All right," Joe said. And they went to the coach.

"I'm not surprised," Coach Venuti told

them both. "In fact, I thought you'd want the signals before the last game."

"I thought about it," Joe said, "but I wanted to show everybody that the Cub game wasn't a fluke. That's all."

So the coach gave them a signal system. "One finger is a fast ball. That's the way the major leaguers play it. One is a fast ball, two is a curve, three is a slider. But you don't throw curves or sliders. You're not supposed to yet. Hurt your arm."

"How do you get him to change speeds?" Betcha asked.

"You put down one finger, for the fast ball, and wiggle it. Wiggling always means off-speed. Two fingers and a wiggle, to the major leagues, means an off-speed curve."

"So that's all?" Betcha asked.

"Not quite," replied the coach. "Remember, you have to signal inside or outside, high or low. You signal inside by pointing with your thumb. Outside, by pointing with your little finger. So a slow ball, inside, is: one finger, a wiggle, and your thumb."

"Okay," said Betcha.

"But one more thing. Don't let the coach of the other team spot what you're doing. Keep the signals between your legs. And especially the wiggle. Wiggle your finger — not your hand. Anybody could see a wiggling hand."

"And if I think he's wrong?" asked Joe.

"Just shake your head. And then, Betcha, you have to give him another signal. The final decision is up to the pitcher. I don't want to see any fights out there."

11

IT MAY BE HARD to believe, but Gale Southworth almost lost the Ranger game for the
Blazers, even though the Blazers were
playing the White Sox.

It's a little complicated, but it went like
this.

The White Sox were having a bad day,
probably because Joe and Betcha were
having a good one. Betcha wiggled, and Joe
threw, and Betcha pointed, and Joe threw
again, and they were fine. The Blazers
jumped off to a 4–0 lead in the second
inning.

Gale, of course, as always, was in the

stands. And J.C., playing first base as he always did when he wasn't pitching, was posing, patting down his hair, and showing her his profile.

In the top of the fourth, Joe threw a super slow ball, because Betcha wiggled harder than ever before, and the White Sox hitter, lunging, popped it up between first and second. Phantom Baxter Snow called for it, waved his arms, circled, waved some more. But J.C. either didn't hear him, or decided that this was a good time to show off. In that last second, he yelled "mine!"

It is a simple law of science. Two ball players can not occupy the same space under a pop-up at the same time.

The collision was awful. Phantom's head hit J.C.'s head. Both went down hard. Neither caught the ball.

Such things happen in baseball. Usually, nobody is really hurt, but you never know. Coach Venuti ran out on the field to

his two injured ball players who were writhing on the ground.

And as he ran, a screech from the stands. It was Gale.

"Oh my God," she cried. *"They've hurt Baxter!"*

You wouldn't think J.C. could have heard that, but he did. He sat bolt upright, hand still on head, and almost yelled back at Gale. *"BAXTER?"* he cried, *"BAXTER?"* And then, he fainted back again, maybe this time for real.

It took maybe half a minute to find out that Phantom was okay. And it took another two minutes before J.C. got up. He staggered, but probably not from the blow on his head.

The rest of the White Sox game was nothing. The Blazers won it easily.

12

THE RANGER GAME was coming up, and two things about it were important. First, it was the Rangers who had given the Blazers that terrible 14–1 shellacking — way back when the Blazers didn't know they were winners.

And second, how would J.C. handle the fact that it was Phantom Baxter Snow, and not him, whom Gale had been watching all season?

J.C. reacted, all right. When he showed up on the field to pitch, his uniform shirt was out of his pants, and one sock was up, the other down around his ankles. His hat was crooked. If he had been an adult, people would have thought he was drunk.

And in his warmups, he was throwing slow junk to spots — imitating Joe Ferguson's style. He wouldn't throw his fast ball.

Coach Venuti was worried. "Get hold of yourself, J.C. This is a good team you have to beat today." J.C. nodded his head, as he went out to the mound, but he didn't pull his socks up.

The Rangers got three runs in the first. J.C., throwing slow, and then still slower, could not hit the spots the way Joe did, and he was pounded. If it hadn't been for Roger's single, Phantom's single, and Betcha's home run, the Blazers would have been on the way to another loss.

By the third inning, the score was 6–6 and J.C. had given up more runs than he had in the entire season. And he still wouldn't go to the fast ball. The one thing that J.C.'s pitching did was to prove to the

Blazers just how good Joe Ferguson really was.

Irky doubled, and scored on Joe's hit. Bunky, the new shortstop, walked, stole second, and scored on Phantom's second hit. All in all, the Blazers got up to nine runs by the end of the fourth, but it still wasn't enough.

With J.C. throwing high when he wanted to throw low, throwing inside when he wanted to throw outside, and mixing poorly, the Rangers were back in the ball game with three runs of their own, and after five full, the score was 9–9.

J.C. struck out to begin the last inning. But a walk, an error, and a blooper gave the Blazers one more run.

And then, in the bottom of the sixth, eight straight pitches, all slow, all balls, and the Rangers had two on with nobody out. Coach Venuti walked slowly to the mound.

"I'm taking you out, J.C.," he told him, as he waved for Phantom to join him on the mound. He couldn't use Joe Ferguson in relief. It was against the league rules to use the same pitcher twice in the same week.

Baxter arrived at the mound and the coach told him he was pitching.

"You must be kidding," Phantom said. "I've never pitched in my life!"

"You're not going to let *him* pitch, are you?" J.C. asked. He looked up in the stands and saw Gale Southworth jumping up and down, in true cheerleader style, for the new pitcher.

"We've got to do something," the coach said. "You're going to lose this game for us . . . over a girl!"

"No, I won't," J.C. said, emphatically. "Let me stay in, Coach. Just watch."

Coach Venuti looked at a now determined J.C. He looked at the Phantom. Looked up to heaven, and said, "All right.

One more batter. Then, we'll see." And he handed J.C. the ball again.

Baxter trotted out back to second base; J. C. straightened his hat.

J.C. threw nine straight fast balls and the game was over. They were all strikes. They were all at the knees. And the Rangers never saw them.

The Blazers had won 10–9, in a game that Gale had almost lost for them.

13

THE MEETING at the practice was short and sweet.

"The Cubs lost another one," Coach Venuti announced. "The Blazers are now tied for first place. Three more wins and we're champions."

"Unless the Cubs win three more, too," Irky corrected.

"Not possible," said the coach. "One of their games is with us!"

And so, the chips were down. Pirates, Cubs, Phillies. Three wins and it was all over. The pitching rotation was perfect. Joe Ferguson for the Pirates, then J.C. for the

Cubs, and then Joe finishes up with the Phillies.

But no one counted on the rain.

The Pirates game was easy. Joe and Betcha mixed nothing with nothing, but spotted it well, and came up winners. Joe had learned that even his poor fast ball was good enough if the batters weren't expecting it.

But the night before the Cubs game, it rained. And in the morning, it was still raining. And then, in the afternoon, it rained some more.

So the league president canceled the game. It was moved to the end of the season, *after* the Phillies game. And in a way, that was fine. The two best clubs playing one final game for the championship.

But, in another way, it was disaster for the Blazers. Because of the pitching rotation. Joe had pitched the Pirates game, and that meant J.C. would have to pitch the next game, no matter who the opponent was. So J.C. would pitch the Phillies game, and Joe — slow-ball Joe — would be going against the Cubs for the championship.

It also meant that the best Cub pitcher — the one who had beaten the Blazers once before — would once again be throwing for the Cubs.

Coach Venuti called the Cub manager. Would the Cubs, he asked, be willing to postpone the makeup game until the week after? They would not. Would the Cubs consider ignoring the pitching rules? They would not. Weren't the Cubs interested in the best possible game between the best two teams? Didn't they want to beat the best Blazer pitcher? The Cubs' manager laughed.

So J.C. pitched the Phillies game, and the Blazers won it easily. J.C. was almost his old self. He threw his fast ball better than ever, but he had learned something from Joe. Now, mixed with that fast ball, was an occasional change of pace — a changeup — that he tried to spot wherever Betcha held his mitt.

But it was more than just J.C. who was effective in the Phillies game. Coach Venuti, in his last look at his collection of "losers" before the championship game, smiled with satisfaction.

Roger, for example, turned out to be a pretty fair outfielder. He still had that weak arm, but he also had speed, and excellent fly-ball judgment. He was confident out there, and Coach Venuti knew he was happier. The coach made a silent bet with himself. He bet that Roger was doing better in school these days.

Roger's father had not telephoned again. He showed up at all the games, of course. But now, he sat silently in the corner of the stands, watching the team play. And after the games, he avoided going near the bench as he had before.

Irky actually looked slimmer. The coach didn't know if he had really lost any weight, or how much, but he was more mobile. He could move. And he no longer brought a sandwich to the games. Nobody on the team ever mentioned the incident with his mother, and that must have pleased him, too.

Phantom Baxter Snow was okay, too, the coach thought. He was still a show boat. He still made "phantom" plays in the practices, and still made every play look harder than it really was. But he was making very few errors now, and hitting well. And combing his hair carefully.

Betcha relaxed. His signal system was working fine, and his guessing on the batters was excellent. He pointed, and wiggled, and laughed a lot. He and Joe were not exactly best friends, but they were team-mates. They helped each other, and that won ball games.

And Joe, himself, had no more complaints. Not once during the past few weeks did he complain of a sore arm, or sore shoulders, or little pains here and little pains there. It was like a magic drug. A few wins were all he needed.

J.C. had fully recovered from the Gale Southworth incident. He had, after all, never actually spoken to Gale. It wasn't as if they were going together. And if Gale preferred Phantom, J.C. thought, well, that was her hard luck.

So win or lose the Cub game, Coach Venuti thought it had been a pretty good season.

14

THE CUBS, the Cubs, the Cubs.

The Blazers were 11 wins, 2 losses. The Cubs were 11 wins, 2 losses.

Last game of the season for both of them. Tied for first place. It was as if someone were writing a TV show, looking for the perfect ending.

But it wasn't perfect. The luck of the rain was against the Blazers.

Because of the rain, and the pitching rules, the BIG CUB PITCHER was going to pitch again. And the Blazers would have to go with Joe Ferguson, even though J.C.

had the great fast ball. The luck of the rain.

Still, this is what you wanted, Coach Venuti mused. The two best teams in one final shootout for the championship. A test of character.

He wasn't so sure he was going to win the test, though. When the two teams were warming up, Joe came to the coach and told him his arm was sore. "Just a little," he said, "right here between the elbow and the shoulder."

Betcha came to the rescue. He acted as if he was taking Joe seriously. "Betcha I can fix it," he told him, and began to rub the arm gently, massaging the muscle. They sat together on the bench, Betcha rubbing, Joe showing him where. In a few minutes, Joe was up throwing, and another crisis had passed.

The Town of Copley, of course, knew about the big game. The local newspaper had blown it up to "World Series" status, and the stands began filling up early. The commissioner of Copley Youth Baseball was there, as well as the league president, as well as the chief of police.

Mrs. Jacobson came to the game. Coach Venuti thought he saw a sandwich, neatly wrapped in wax paper, behind her purse. But to give her credit, she never offered it to Irky.

And, of course, Roger's father was there. And Gale Southworth. And another girl with Gale Southworth. Phantom and J.C. were over talking to them before the game, both awkward, both patting their hair. Both looked as neat as any Blazer would ever look.

Coach Venuti took the team behind the stands for his final pep talk.

"Well," he began, "here we are. In the championship game. You made it. I'm terribly proud of you. But I also want you to

know that this last game is *not that impor- tant!*" He paused.

"Someone's going to win, and someone's going to lose. Nobody deserves to lose a game like this. But it's only a game. It isn't a matter of life and death.

"I want you guys to go out there and have fun. Play the game, but enjoy it. If anyone is going to get nervous, let it be the other team."

"Don't you want us to win?" asked Betcha.

The old question. Do I want them to win? Is winning important? The coach smiled. "In my book," Coach Venuti said, "you've already won. Every one of you is a winner. Remember that. Sure. If you win this last one, well, fine. But if you lose it, don't hang your heads. You were all great to get this far. You guys have had a wonderful year. I've had a wonderful year. You're already champions."

"I'd still like to win this one," J.C. said, a little confused.

"Me too," Roger chimed in. Everybody looked at him. Roger almost never said anything. But he was a team player, now.

The team broke, and returned to the field for "The Star-Spangled Banner." Every seat in the stands was filled.

15

THE CUB PITCHER was good. Really good. Everything he did in that first game, he did again in this one. Fast. Low. Clever. The Blazers were having a terrible time getting anyone on base.

But Joe Ferguson matched him, inning for inning, at the start. He had the Cub hitters swinging off stride, lunging at slow pitches, and handcuffed by the fast ones. It was as if they could never tell when Joe was going to throw fast.

It was 0–0 after three and a half innings . . . just like a championship game should be.

Then, the Cubs got on to something. After three of Joe's pitches to the first batter in the bottom of the fourth, the Cubs' first-base coach stage-whispered "change!" Joe threw a changeup, just as Betcha had signaled, and the Cub hitter slashed the ball to deep left field. Roger made a fine catch for the out.

Again, with the second hitter of the inning, the Cub coach stage-whispered "change!" just before Joe threw his changeup, and again, a Cub hitter timed it perfectly. The Blazer centerfielder caught the long drive on the run, right in front of the wall.

And then, the next Cub hitter hit one out of the park. Over the fence. Home run.

The Cubs weren't swinging at Joe's fast ball. They were just standing there, waiting for the changeup. And because of that first-base coach, they seemed to know every time it was coming.

The inning was finally over, but the

Cubs had hit three pitches really hard, and had a run.

"They're guessing right," Joe complained. "Every time I used my slow ball, they were waiting for it."

Coach Venuti pulled his pitcher and catcher to the corner of the bench. "They're not guessing," the coach told them. "They're reading Betcha's signals. When he wiggles his finger for the changeup, he's wiggling a little of his wrist, too. And they know what that wiggle means."

"Let's change signals," Betcha said.

"Yeah," said Coach Venuti. "But let's change them in a certain way. From now on, one finger is still the fast ball. But now, two fingers means changeup. The wiggle doesn't mean anything." And he turned to the rest of the team. "Let's get some runs, you guys!" He clapped his hands.

Roger walked, but after two strikeouts, he was still on first base. And then . . . and then the miracle that the Blazers were

waiting for. The Cub pitcher reared back and fired his best fast ball, over the heart of the plate, waist high.

Phantom Baxter Snow, who had been pretending all year, took his marvelous imaginary swing — but this time, it was real. This time, for the first time in his life, the ball really did jump off his bat, flying on a high arc for the distant fence. And when Phantom shielded his eyes from the sun to watch — as he had done for thousands of imaginary home runs before — this time, he really did see the flight of the ball out, out, out over the wall. His dream — his thousand dreams — had come true.

Home run. Home run. The Blazers were leading 2–1.

And Gale Southworth was beside herself.

But the game was not over. The Cubs still had two more times at bat.

16

BETCHA WAS A very smart catcher.

Guessing that the Cubs were still laying back, waiting for the changeup, he called three straight fast balls on the first hitter in the bottom of the fifth inning. The batter took them all, and was called out on strikes. One out.

He could see the Cub coach talking furiously to his next batter, as he stepped up to the plate. The coach was pleading with him to swing the bat!

Joe got lucky. He threw a medium-fast ball on the first pitch, the Cub swung, and lifted a harmless pop fly to Phantom at second base. Phantom waved wildly, yelled, circled, waved some more, and then made the catch. Two out.

But what Betcha did to that third batter of the inning was worth the season. He was one of their heavy hitters, and he fouled the first pitch deep into left field. But foul is foul, and it was just a long strike.

Joe's next pitch was a fast ball, right on the corner. The umpire called it strike two.

And then . . .

Betcha put one finger down for the fast ball, and then, remembering it didn't mean anything any more . . . he wiggled. The Cub first-base coach stage-whispered "change!" The Cub hitter got ready for the slow ball, and Joe Ferguson reared back and threw the hardest fast ball of his entire life.

The Cub hitter looked surprised. He hardly got the bat off his shoulder, as he tried a futile poke at the ball. But it was too late. The ball was in Betcha's mitt. Strike three.

Three out.

Betcha was laughing out loud when he came back to the bench. He, at least, was taking the coach's advice. He was having fun.

There never was a sixth inning like the sixth inning of the Cub–Blazer game. It was unbelievable.

First of all, the Blazers did nothing in their half of the sixth. And the Cubs came to bat one more time, trailing by one run. This was their last licks. Unless they scored, the Blazers were the champs.

The first Cub walked. The second Cub grounded to Bunky at shortstop, who flipped the ball to Phantom at second, for the force out. One out, man on first.

The next Cub doubled, putting men on second and third, one out. But the batter after him popped up, so there were two outs. Coach Venuti strolled out to the mound.

"Look, Joe," he said, trying to keep calm, "this guy coming up is the big Cub pitcher, and he's a pretty good hitter, too. First base is open. Why don't we put him on base on purpose? Then, they'll have the bases loaded, so we have a force at any base."

Joe nodded, and when Coach Venuti returned to the bench, he threw four wide pitches deliberately, and walked the bases full.

And that's when the confusion started.

Bases loaded, two out, last of the sixth, championship game. Joe threw a fast ball. The hitter leaned in and slammed it, on the line, to left centerfield. A clean hit. The Cub on third scored easily. The Cub who was on second, running at the crack of the bat, rounded third and also scored before Roger had even recovered the ball. That, of course, was the winning run.

But the big Cub pitcher on first, knowing that his run "didn't matter," just stood between first and second bases. And when he saw his team-mate from second going all the way home, he leaped into the air and clapped his hands. He then held up his first finger in a victory salute! He didn't bother running to second base.

The stands emptied on to the field. The Cub pitcher's father ran to him and hugged him. His mother danced around him. He was jumping for joy.

Roger, in deep left field, realized something that nobody else did. He knew that if he got the ball to second base before the Cub pitcher got there, then it would simply be a force out, three outs, and the runs wouldn't count. He yelled to Phantom, and then . . . threw a floating fly ball, way over his head.

The fans were now milling around the infield, lifting the Cubs, dancing, cheering. The overthrown baseball, therefore, went into the crowd, where it was picked up by a fan. Fathers, mothers, girl friends, little kids were running all over the place.

From deep left field, Roger came running into the crowd, looking for the ball. He elbowed his way past the screaming fans and found the fan, who had put the ball in his pocket.

"Give me the ball," Roger demanded, angrily.

"Why?" said the fan, as he took it out of his pocket, and held it aloft. "It's a souvenir!"

Roger swung just once. He hit the surprised fan in the belly. The fan doubled over and dropped the ball.

Roger picked it up, and taking no chances with the crowd, ran himself, dodging the fans, over to second base. He jumped on the base with both feet, held the ball up, and looked for the umpire.

The umpire was right there. He had watched the whole thing. He raised his

right fist, and shouted to be heard over the crowd.

"Out! The runner is *OUT* going to second."

And now, only Roger and the umpire knew that the Blazers had won the championship. For if the runner was out going to second, then it was a simple force play, and none of the runs counted. The Cub on first had to reach second, and he never did. It was three out. The Blazers had won. The game, and the season, was over.

It was the greatest goof in the history of Copley baseball.

It was the goof that won the pennant . . . for the Blazers!

It was awful. The shouting and the screaming. The Cub manager was beside himself. The Cub pitcher, who had failed to go to second, was arguing furiously with the umpire.

The Cub manager appealed the play to

the league president. And then, to the commissioner. The chief of police positioned himself next to the umpire, just in case things got rough.

But the rule is the rule. The runner was forced out. None of the runs counted. The Blazers had won, 2–1. The Blazers were the champs.

And once the Blazers, and their fans, realized what had happened, the riot started all over again. This time, it was the Blazers who were dancing, and shouting, and carrying on. Roger was picked up by Betcha, and J.C., and Irky, and pounded on the back until he cried through his laughter.

Bunky and Joe and Phantom, who was a hero himself, jumped on the pyramid, and they all came tumbling down.

No one cared. They lay there, on the ground, pounding each other with hats and gloves, and bare hands.

Gale Southworth kissed Roger.

Irky's mother, still confused about what it was all about, threw away the sandwich and hugged her son.

The Blazers had won the championship.

The Blazers!

Late that evening, Coach Paul Venuti had an idea.

"I think I'll call *him*," he said to himself, smiling. He walked to the phone.

Author's Note

ON SEPTEMBER 23, 1908, the second-place Chicago Cubs were in New York for a crucial game with the first-place New York Giants. The Cubs were less than half a game behind the Giants in the standings.

The score was 1–1 going into the last half of the ninth inning. There were two outs, Moose McCormick was on third, and 19-year-old Fred Merkle was on first. Al Bridwell lashed a Jack Pfiester pitch to centerfield for a clean single, scoring McCormick and apparently ending the game with the Giants winning, 2–1.

Merkle, halfway to second, watched

McCormick score and, without touching second base, sprinted for the clubhouse. 25,000 Giant fans streamed onto the playing field to celebrate their victory.

Johnny Evers, the Cub second baseman, knew Merkle had not touched second. He called to centerfielder Solly Hofman to throw him the ball, but Hofman, confused by the crowd, overthrew. Giant first-base coach Joe McGinnity, realizing what was happening, outwrestled Cub shortstop Joe Tinker for the ball, and threw it away.

Floyd Kroh, a Cub relief pitcher who wasn't even in the game, saw a fan pick up the ball. He demanded the ball, and when the fan refused, he knocked him cold, took the ball, and ran to give it to Evers, still on second base. Umpire Hank O'Day called Merkle out for failing to touch second, disallowed the run, and immediately called the game for darkness, ending it as a 1–1 tie.

The Cubs and the Giants finished the

season with identical records of 98 wins, 55 losses, 1 tie.

The tie was rescheduled, and the Cubs beat the Giants 4–2, which gave the Cubs the pennant.

If Merkle had touched second base, of course, the Giants would have finished a game ahead of the Cubs, and *they* would have won the pennant.

Merkle's failure to touch second base was, and still is, considered the greatest goof in the history of the game.